The Great Pig Escape

Written and illustrated by

Eileen Christelow

CLARION BOOKS/*New York*

Bert and Ethel lived on a small farm. They grew the best lettuce, peas, tomatoes, corn, and turnips for miles around.

One day, when they were out hoeing weeds, Bert said, "I've been thinking we should raise a few pigs."

"Sounds like trouble to me," said Ethel. "I'd rather stick with turnips."

But Bert bought six little piglets anyway.

"They look like more trouble than turnips," said Ethel. "But they are kind of cute."

"They won't be cute for long," said Bert. "Eight months from now they'll be pork chops, so don't go falling in love with them."

"Sh-h-h!" said Ethel. "You shouldn't say things like that. You'll upset them."

Over the next few months, the piglets grew into pigs. They spent their days grubbing, rooting, snuffling, and wallowing. And they grew fatter every week.

One day, when the pigs were slurping up their slop, Bert said to Ethel, "I think these pigs are big enough to sell at the market tomorrow."

"Sh-h-h!" said Ethel. "They'll hear you!"

Sure enough, the pigs stopped slurping.

"Oink???" said one.

"Oink!!!" squealed another.

That night, there was a lot of oinking in the pigpen.
"What's got into those pigs?" grumbled Bert.
"Sounds like they're planning something," said Ethel.
"Don't be ridiculous!" said Bert.

The next morning, the pigs ran this way and that way. They oinked and they squealed and they shrieked. Bert and Ethel had to ask the neighbors to help them load the pigs into the back of the truck.

"Where did you put the bolt that locks the tailgate?" panted Ethel.
"On the ground," puffed Bert.
"I don't see it," said Ethel.

No one could find the bolt. They had to tie the tailgates together with rope.

Then Bert and Ethel got into the truck, rolled up the windows, and turned on the radio, so they couldn't hear the oinking and squealing and shrieking. They also couldn't hear the pigs chewing on the rope.

As they bumped and rattled down the road toward town,
the rope snapped. The tailgates flapped open.
But Bert and Ethel didn't notice.

At the edge of town, Bert and Ethel stopped for gas at Thelma's Garage. The radio was still rocking and rolling and wailing. And the pigs were still oinking and squealing.

No one noticed when two pigs scrambled from the back of the truck and scooted under a nearby fence.

Bert and Ethel made another quick stop at the Food Co-op
for soda and sandwiches.

On the other side of town, Bert and Ethel had to stop at a train crossing while a long, long freight train clattered by.

"It's going to take all day to get these pigs to the market," grumbled Bert.

"Maybe you should check on them," said Ethel.

"No need," said Bert. "I'm sure they're fine."

20

When they finally arrived at the auction yard, Bert got out of the truck and went to check on the pigs.

"They're GONE!" he cried.

"What?" said Ethel.

"The pigs!" shouted Bert. "They got away!"

He jumped back into the truck and they hightailed it back down the road to look for the pigs.

At the railroad crossing, Bert and Ethel saw two hitchhikers.
"Have you seen any pigs around here?" called Ethel.
The two hitchhikers grunted and shook their heads from side to side.

Bert and Ethel tore into town and parked the truck.

No one at the Food Co-op or at Rose's Second Hand Clothes had seen any pigs.

"But I'd like to find the person who took the clothes off my sidewalk display," said Rose.

Bert and Ethel searched up and down Main Street. They asked everyone they saw, "Have you seen our pigs?"

Ethel stopped at Thelma's Garage.
"I haven't seen any pigs," Thelma said. "But someone just stole the wash off my line . . . including my favorite dress with the purple flowers!"

Bert met the farmer from over by the railroad crossing.
"I haven't seen any pigs," said the farmer. "But I'm looking
for the scoundrel who took the clothes off my scarecrows."
Pretty soon, people all over town were helping to look for
the missing hats, pants, dresses, shirts . . . and pigs.

Ethel searched down by the bus station.

"You don't usually see pigs around here," said the bus driver.
"But I'll keep an eye out for them."

As he was talking to Ethel, several passengers slipped onto the
bus without tickets.

No one could find the hats, pants, dresses, shirts
. . . or pigs.
"How can six pigs just disappear?" groaned Bert.
"I told you they were planning something," said Ethel.
"Impossible!" said Bert. "They're only pigs!"

Bert and Ethel looked for the pigs for several more weeks.
They advertised in the paper. They put up signs. But no one had
seen their pigs.

Finally, one day when they were having coffee in town, Bert
said to Ethel, "I've had it with pigs! From now on I'm sticking
with vegetables."

"We can grow some fine turnips in the pigpen," said Ethel.

Then one day several months later . . .

. . . the post office received a large box from Florida addressed to:

The people missing hats, pants, dresses, shirts . . . and pigs.

Bert and Ethel hurried down to the post office. The people who were missing clothes were already there.

"Well I'll be," said Thelma. "Here is my dress with the purple flowers—washed, ironed, and folded neat as can be! Now who can figure that?"

"What do you have for the people missing pigs?" asked Bert.

"Just a postcard," said the postmaster.

"Who sent us a postcard?" said Ethel.

On the front of the postcard was a picture of a sunset on a Florida beach.

On the other side, it said,